GORILLAS
IN OUR MIDST

GORILLAS
IN OUR MIDST

Richard Fairgray and Terry Jones

Coloring by Tara Black

Sky Pony Press
New York

For Joe and Kenneth

Sky Pony Press books may be purchased in bulk at special discounts for sales promotion, corporate gifts, fund-raising, or educational purposes. Special editions can also be created to specifications. For details, contact the Special Sales Department, Sky Pony Press, 307 West 36th Street, 11th Floor, New York, NY 10018 or info@skyhorsepublishing.com.

Sky Pony® is a registered trademark of Skyhorse Publishing, Inc.®, a Delaware corporation.

Visit our website at www.skyponypress.com.

10 9 8 7 6 5 4 3 2

Manufactured in the United States of America, October 2015
This product conforms to CPSIA 2008

Library of Congress Cataloging-in-Publication Data is available on file.

Cover design by Danielle Ceccolini
Cover illustration credit Richard Fairgray

Print ISBN: 978-1-63220-607-7
Ebook ISBN: 978-1-63220-837-8

You know what they always say: "You should always carry a banana with you."

Because you never know when there might be a gorilla around.

Gorillas can be hard to spot. They are masters of disguise.

Plus, they're really good at hiding.

Gorillas often get jobs that let them wear masks. Like a surgeon . . .

or an astronaut . . .

or a ninja . . .

or a SCUBA diver.

Gorillas have been in our midst for a long time now. Surely you've heard of Gorilliam Shakespeare?

Or Apebraham Lincoln?

Some gorillas have even taught people sign language.

Not all gorillas are grown-ups, of course.
There are even some gorillas at my school.

That's why no one wants to ride the seesaw with Eric.

Gorillas are too big for cars,
so they always take the bus.

Well . . .

except the really cool ones.

You may think you've seen a gorilla swinging through your town.

But ten to one it's just an orangutan. They're terrible at hiding.

But sometimes even gorillas slip up.

Did she say *book* . . . or *ook*?!

Like I said, always have a
banana with you.

You never know when you might get hungry.

The End